SWARM OF THE FANGED LIZARDS

DINOSAUR COVE™

DINOSAUR COVE™

SWARM OF THE FANGED LIZARDS

by
REX STONE

illustrated by
MIKE SPOOR

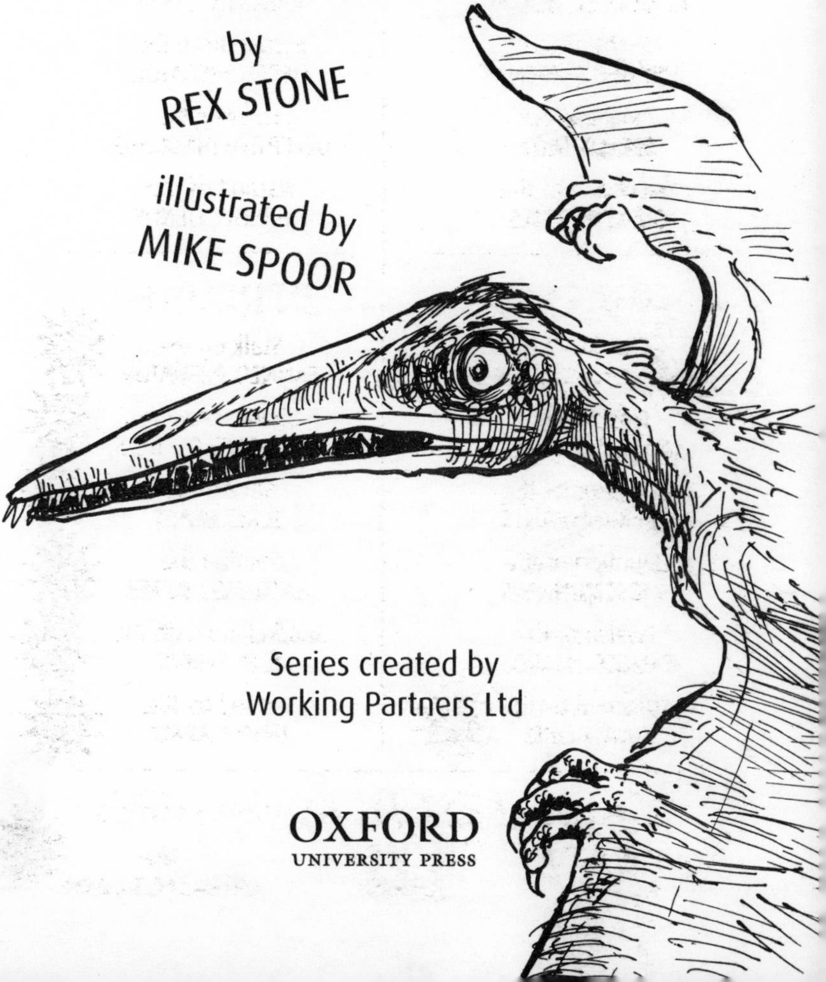

Series created by
Working Partners Ltd

OXFORD
UNIVERSITY PRESS

Special thanks to Jane Clarke

A special **ROAR** for Remy Smet. R.S.

The illustrations in this book are dedicated to Carla, Rasmus and York. M.S.

OXFORD
UNIVERSITY PRESS

Great Clarendon Street, Oxford OX2 6DP

Oxford University Press is a department of the University of Oxford.
It furthers the University's objective of excellence in research, scholarship,
and education by publishing worldwide in

Oxford   New York

Auckland   Cape Town   Dar es Salaam   Hong Kong   Karachi
Kuala Lumpur   Madrid   Melbourne   Mexico City   Nairobi
New Delhi   Shanghai   Taipei   Toronto

With offices in

Argentina   Austria   Brazil   Chile   Czech Republic   France   Greece
Guatemala   Hungary   Italy   Japan   Poland   Portugal   Singapore
South Korea   Switzerland   Thailand   Turkey   Ukraine   Vietnam

Oxford is a registered trade mark of Oxford University Press
in the UK and in certain other countries

British Library Cataloguing in Publication Data

Data available

ISBN: 978-0-19-278988-4

1 3 5 7 9 10 8 6 4 2

Printed in Great Britain
Paper used in the production of this book is a natural,
recyclable product made from wood grown in sustainable forests
The manufacturing process conforms to the environmental
regulations of the country of origin

FACT FILE

➡ JAMIE'S DAD'S MUSEUM ON THE BOTTOM FLOOR OF THE LIGHTHOUSE IN DINOSAUR COVE IS THE SECOND BEST PLACE IN THE WORLD TO BE. THE FIRST IS DINO WORLD, OF COURSE, THE SECRET THAT JAMIE AND HIS BEST FRIEND TOM HAVE DISCOVERED IN THE BACK OF A DEEP, DARK CAVE. BUT ESCAPING TO THE TRIASSIC ISN'T ALWAYS THE DRY, HOT ADVENTURE THAT THE BOYS EXPECT.

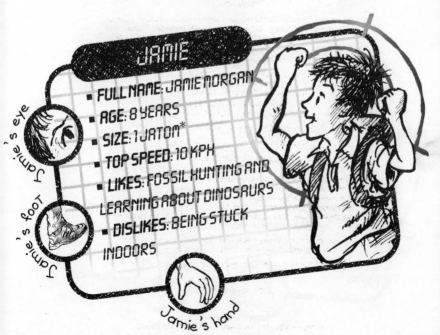

JAMIE

- FULL NAME: JAMIE MORGAN
- AGE: 8 YEARS
- SIZE: 1 JATOM*
- TOP SPEED: 10 KPH
- LIKES: FOSSIL HUNTING AND LEARNING ABOUT DINOSAURS
- DISLIKES: BEING STUCK INDOORS

Jamie's eye

Jamie's foot

Jamie's hand

*NOTE: A JATOM IS THE SIZE OF JAMIE OR TOM: 125 CM TALL AND 27 KG IN WEIGHT

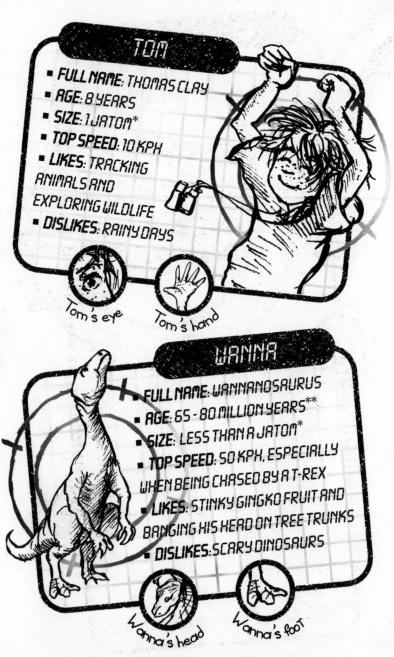

TOM
- **FULL NAME:** THOMAS CLAY
- **AGE:** 8 YEARS
- **SIZE:** 1 JATOM*
- **TOP SPEED:** 10 KPH
- **LIKES:** TRACKING ANIMALS AND EXPLORING WILDLIFE
- **DISLIKES:** RAINY DAYS

Tom's eye

Tom's hand

WANNA
- **FULL NAME:** WANNANOSAURUS
- **AGE:** 65 - 80 MILLION YEARS**
- **SIZE:** LESS THAN A JATOM*
- **TOP SPEED:** 50 KPH, ESPECIALLY WHEN BEING CHASED BY A T-REX
- **LIKES:** STINKY GINGKO FRUIT AND BANGING HIS HEAD ON TREE TRUNKS
- **DISLIKES:** SCARY DINOSAURS

Wanna's head

Wanna's foot

*NOTE: A JATOM IS THE SIZE OF JAMIE OR TOM: 125 CM TALL AND 27 KG IN WEIGHT
**NOTE: SCIENTISTS CALL THIS PERIOD THE LATE CRETACEOUS

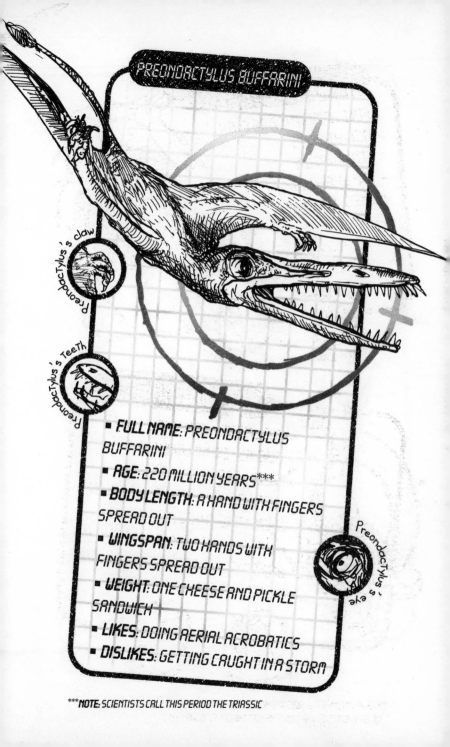

PREONDACTYLUS BUFFARINI

- **FULL NAME:** PREONDACTYLUS BUFFARINI
- **AGE:** 220 MILLION YEARS***
- **BODY LENGTH:** A HAND WITH FINGERS SPREAD OUT
- **WINGSPAN:** TWO HANDS WITH FINGERS SPREAD OUT
- **WEIGHT:** ONE CHEESE AND PICKLE SANDWICH
- **LIKES:** DOING AERIAL ACROBATICS
- **DISLIKES:** GETTING CAUGHT IN A STORM

Preondactylus's claw

Preondactylus's teeth

Preondactylus's eye

***NOTE: SCIENTISTS CALL THIS PERIOD THE TRIASSIC

Village

Marina

Sealight Head

8

Landslips where
clay and fossils are

gh Tide beach line

Low Tide beach line

DINO CAVE

Smuggler's Point

Sea

'What's the big secret?' Tom Clay asked his best friend Jamie Morgan. 'Why did your grandad tell us to come up here?'

The boys had just climbed the spiral steps to the lantern room balcony right at the top of the old lighthouse where Jamie lived with his dad and grandad.

'He wouldn't say,' Jamie replied. 'Wish he'd hurry and catch us up, I'm getting soggy.' He peered into the cold grey drizzle that surrounded them. 'On a sunny day,

you can see all of Dinosaur Cove from here,' he said.

'Everything except our cave,' replied Tom. 'You couldn't see that, even with a telescope on a clear day.'

The two friends grinned at each other. Hidden away in Dinosaur Cove was a cave that no one else knew about. It led to an amazing world of stomping, chomping dinosaurs and other awesome prehistoric beasts.

That was their big secret, but what was Grandad's?

Behind them, the small iron-framed glass door of the lantern room creaked open. Grandad squeezed out onto the balcony, puffing and panting. He was wearing his bright yellow oilskin hat.

'A hundred and seventy-two steps,' Grandad spluttered.

'But it's worth it to see this. And I don't mean the view! Keep very quiet, me hearties. We don't want 'em to hear us . . .'

Grandad put his finger to his lips and tiptoed round the balcony. Jamie and Tom shrugged at each other and followed.

'See?' he hissed, prodding a pudding-sized pile of grey gritty stuff with his foot.

Jamie glanced at Tom. Tom raised his eyebrows.

'Looks like a heap of mucky rice crispies to me,' he muttered.

Grandad pointed up at the lighthouse roof. Jamie and Tom followed his gaze.

There, under the eaves of the sloping

roof, directly above the
pile of grey stuff, was a
little hole where the wood
had rotted. It seemed to have
something curled up inside it.

'See our new house guests?' Grandad
whispered. 'They've made themselves
very comfortable.'

Tom put his binoculars to his eyes and
focused them on the hole.

'Bats!' he breathed. 'Two of them hanging
upside down, fast asleep.'

Jamie glanced down at the grey gritty stuff.
'So that's bat poo,' he chuckled. 'It looks
crunchy!'

'These little critters are pipistrelle bats,'
Grandad said in a low voice. 'They eat
insects, so their poo is insect wings and other
bits they can't digest.' He looked at the boys.
'Not scared of bats, are you?'

15

'No!' Jamie and Tom both made a muffled snorting noise. Grandad didn't know it, but they'd met much scarier things than bats on their adventures.

'Some people are terrified of bats.' Grandad smiled.

'That's because they don't know anything about them,' Tom replied. He made his fist into an imaginary microphone. 'Bats,' he whispered, in his best secretly-watching-wildlife TV presenter voice, 'have a sort of radar that stops them bumping into things in the dark. It's called echo location . . . '

'Let me have a look, bat brain!' Jamie hissed. He took the binoculars from Tom and wiped the

water drops off the lenses. The bats w
not much bigger than mice, with pointy ears
and dark furry backs. Their leathery wings
were stretched around their plump tummies

so thin that he could clearly see the long,
bendy bones that supported them like the
spokes of an umbrella. Tiny claws sprouted
from the tips of the wings.

'Just like tiny pterosaurs!' Jamie murmured.

'Bats are mammals, not reptiles like
pterosaurs, you wombat,' Tom whispered.

'I know that, fossil face,' Jamie replied.
'But they're the only mammals that can flap
their wings and fly.'

A gust of wind whirled round the
lighthouse, whipping icy drizzle into their faces.

'Time to go inside,' Grandad said,
hanging onto his hat. 'If I were you,
I'd do what the bats are doing and find
somewhere warm and dry to spend
the rest of the day.' He headed
towards the door to the
lantern room.

Jamie looked
at Tom.

'I know just the
place,' he said.
'Somewhere
much hotter
and drier than
Dinosaur Cove.'

'Somewhere where there are real live pterosaurs to check out,' Tom added.

'Triassic World!' Jamie and Tom said together.

Above them, the bats stirred.

'Better get going before we wake up the guests,' Tom said.

They dashed down the lighthouse steps, grabbed Jamie's backpack as they barrelled through the kitchen, and hurtled down the path to the beach.

'Got the Fossil Finder
and Triassic ammonite?'
Tom puffed as they sprinted
along the beach to the
Smuggler's Cave.

'Check and check!' Jamie panted.

And in no time at all, they'd taken off
their coats and squeezed through the gap at
the back of the cave to the secret chamber.
They placed their feet into the fossilized
dinosaur footprints that ran across the floor.

'Dino World here we come!' Jamie yelled.
He shone his torch towards what looked
like a solid rock wall. Tom counted as they
stepped towards it . . .

'One . . .
two . . .
three . . .
four . . .
five . . .'

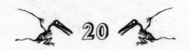

In a blinding flash of light, the smell of dried pine needles filled their nostrils. They were in the ancient hollowed-out tree in the smouldering heat of Triassic Dino World!

CHAPTER 2

'Ooof!' Jamie gasped. It felt as if all the air had been knocked out of his lungs. He'd been expecting the blistering bone-dry heat of the Triassic, but the air was so hot and wet, it felt as though he'd jumped into a sticky sauna. He peered out of the hollow tree. The tops of the Red Mountains were lost in a murky heat haze, and the sun was a bright orange smudge high in the milky white sky.

'The air's as thick as soup.' Tom coughed.

'Prehistoric soup,' Jamie agreed with a grin. 'P soup for short.'

Tom groaned.

A scaly nose appeared round the edge of the hole in the tree bark, followed by a bony reptilian head.

Grunk!

'Wanna!' Jamie exclaimed. 'You were waiting for us.'

The
boys grinned
at each other.
'Dino World
wouldn't be the same
without you, Wanna,' Tom
said, patting him on the nose.
Wanna lowered his head and
pushed his way into the hollowed
out tree.

Grunk, grunk, grunk!

Wanna was bouncing around between the two boys in the confined space.

'Stop messing about, you bone head,' Tom said. 'It's time for our next adventure.'

But Wanna was too excited about something.

'Calm down, Wanna!' Jamie spluttered as Wanna barged him out into the pine needles.

Then the little dinosaur's scaly tail whacked Tom on the nose as he struggled to turn around. 'Ouch! Thanks Wanna,' Tom groaned as he climbed free.

Wanna poked his head out of the tree and glanced from side to side, grunking nervously. His tail was curled up behind him, with the tip dangling in front of his eyes.

'He's gotten himself all in a twist.' Jamie giggled.

'Wanna's very jumpy,' Tom said with a frown, rubbing his nose. 'That usually means something's going to happen.'

'Like something big and nasty is coming our way,' Jamie agreed. He whirled round.

'I can't see far in this haze,' he grumbled.

Tom examined the ground around the tree. 'No sign of any predator footprints,' he murmured. 'Maybe the change in weather is making Wanna nervous. He seems to be calming down now.'

They stared at Wanna. Their prehistoric friend had stopped grunking. He tiptoed out

of the hollow and squeezed himself between the boys, slowly wagging his tail.

'He's still a bit clingy; we'd better be on our guard,' Jamie told Tom. He rummaged into his backpack and took out the map they'd made of Triassic Dino World.

'Where should we look for pterosaurs?' Tom asked.

'I read that some of them ate fish,' Jamie said. 'So somewhere with water would be a good place to start.'

'The sea's a long way away. Let's check out the pond.' Tom pointed to the spot they'd marked on the map near the foot of the Red Mountains.

Jamie took out his compass and lined up the bearing.

'This way,' he said, pointing into the steamy

heat haze. 'Let's hope the
monster crocs aren't home
this time.' He plunged into
the Triassic forest.

'Wanna's sticking so close,
he's treading on my heels,' Tom
complained as they pushed their way
through the tall horsetails and broad
leaf ferns sprouting curly new fronds.
Everything was growing green and
lush, and the ground beneath their
feet was getting soggier and soggier.

A frog the size and shape of a
football with some of the air let out
flopped across their path, pushing
along its fat body with long skinny

legs. It had lumpy dark orange and green skin and red flashes over its horned eyelids.

Wanna nudged it with his nose. Instead of leaping into the air, the frog scuttled off into the jungle, croaking.

'It's too big and heavy to hop,' Jamie chuckled.

Tom looked thoughtful. 'If frogs are living in the forest,' he said, 'it must've been raining for days.'

'Weeks!' Jamie said, squelching though a patch of gooey mud.

'Months!' Tom sploshed across a puddle.

'Years!' Jamie hopped onto a patch of swampy ferns, then stopped dead. Ahead of him, nestled at the base of the rocky Red

Mountains, was a wide expanse of water with conifer trees growing up out of it.

Tom and Wanna walloped into the back of him.

'That's the pond?' Jamie exclaimed. 'It's much bigger than it was before!'

'The rain has turned it into a lake,' Tom said.

Jamie clambered up on a fallen tree trunk and gazed through the heat haze that hung over the swampy lake.

'No sign of any pterosaurs,' he announced.

'No sign of the monster crocs either,' Tom declared.

'That's good,' Jamie remarked. 'Wanna would make a tasty treat for a postosuchus.'

There was a sudden
splosh!

Grunk!

Wanna leapt into the air

'It's only another frog,' Jamie said.
'There's another . . . and another! It's a
frog gathering.' He pointed to the big fat
orange and green frogs creeping out of the
undergrowth and splashing into the lake.
Wanna sheepishly wagged his tail.

'Do pterosaurs eat frogs?'
Tom wondered.

'Dunno.' Jamie jumped
down from the log he
was standing on. 'Are
there any prehistoric
fish in there?'

splosh!

The boys and Wanna peered into the murky water.

'Can't see any,' Tom murmured. He pointed to what looked like slimy cream-coloured jelly beans rolling around in the swampy shallows. 'What do you reckon these are? Eggs?'

An insect the size of a hornet began to buzz round Jamie's head.

Zzzzzzzzzub!

Jamie swiped it away, relieved to see that it had no sting. It was quickly followed by another and another. With every

passing second, there were more and more
of them. In less than a minute, the hot air
was thick with insects, thrumming with their
buzzy silver wings. Jamie thrashed out, feeling
insect wings flutter against his hands and arms
as he slapped them away. Beside him, Tom
was doing the same and Wanna was grunking
and lashing the insects with his tail.

'Where are they coming from?' Jamie
asked, looking up into the mist.

'Those slimy eggs on the lake,' Tom said.
'They're hatching out, like giant mayflies.'

All around the lake shore, the insects
were launching themselves into the air.

Then Triassic frogs of all sizes,
from little ones that hadn't lost their
tadpole tails, to big ones like half-
deflated beach balls, were crawling out of
the undergrowth. They lined the shallows,
catching the insects in their
wide mouths.

'It's a frog feast.' Jamie laughed.

'They must have known about the hatching,' Tom agreed. 'Look! They're even using their thumbs to cram the insects down their throats.'

'The greedy guts are as bad as a you-know-what-asaurus with stinky gingko fruit.' Jamie glanced at Wanna. Their wannanosaurus friend had his head to one side and was gazing up at the milky sky.

Jamie nudged Tom.

'He senses something,' Tom murmured.

'More insects?' Jamie guessed. But as he said it, he heard a strange flapping noise above the buzzing insects and the croaking frogs. The frogs heard it, too. They splashed into the lake and disappeared beneath the surface.

A huge shadow darkened the sky. Wanna began to whimper as the air filled with the sound of beating wings. Jamie wrapped his arms around his head as a cloud of bat-like creatures broke

through the mist.
The creatures were
swooping towards them,
aiming their beaks like arrow
heads.

'Pterosaurs!' Tom yelled.
'Take cover!'

CHAPTER 3

Jamie, Tom, and Wanna ducked down behind
the fallen tree trunk and peered into the sky.
The swarm of small pterosaurs was flitting and
darting over the water.

'They're only the size of magpies,' Jamie
realized. 'Don't be a scaredy-saurus, Wanna;
these ones are much too small to carry you off.'

He watched the pterosaurs whirling
and circling in a blur of leathery wings,
miraculously not crashing into each other.

'Awesome flying!' he breathed.

 41

Tom examined the scene through his binoculars. 'They're moving so fast it's hard to see what they're doing,' he commented, 'but they're not fishing.'

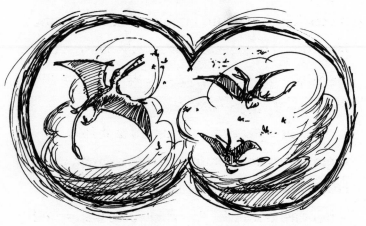

'They're catching the insects,' Jamie said. 'It's a feeding frenzy!'

Tom let the binoculars dangle round his neck. 'Don't move,' he hissed. 'One's coming down to land.'

They watched the pterosaur circle down from the sky on its leathery wings. It was covered in blue-grey velvety fur with creamy

speckles, and it had a long whip-like tail with a kite-shaped tag of skin on the end.

Jamie held his breath as it landed on the log right in front of him. It was so close that he could see the thin bendy bones supporting its wings. There were four needle-sharp fangs sticking out from the front of its beak, which was stuffed full of insects.

The pterosaur's wings rustled as it folded them across its back. It sat for a moment, crunching up the insects it had caught. Then it hobbled down the log, flapped its wings, and lumbered into the air.

'They're great fliers, but not as good as birds at walking or take-off,' Tom remarked. 'I reckon these pterosaurs must live high up. They'd get eaten if they nested on the ground. What does the Fossil Finder say?'

'I'll check.' Jamie flipped it open. The Happy Hunting screen popped up and he typed in *TRIASSIC PTEROSAURS*. He quickly scanned the information that popped up.

'They're called Pre-on-dac-tyl-us Buf-far-in-i,' Jamie said, pronouncing the name carefully. 'The Fossil Finder says *"PALEONTOLOGISTS HAVE BEEN ABLE TO FIND OUT VERY LITTLE ABOUT THE HABITS OF THIS, THE FIRST OF THE PTEROSAURS,"* ' he said, snapping it shut.

'We could tell those scientists a thing or two about buffies.' Tom grinned as they watched the pterosaurs swoop through the air and skim over the water, hunting and gobbling down the insects as they hatched.

Then, suddenly, as if they were one giant creature, the buffies soared up into the sky.

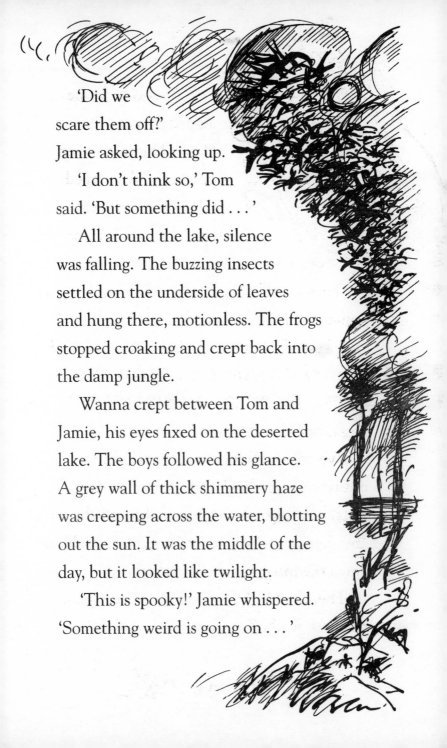

'Did we
scare them off?'
Jamie asked, looking up.

'I don't think so,' Tom
said. 'But something did . . .'

All around the lake, silence
was falling. The buzzing insects
settled on the underside of leaves
and hung there, motionless. The frogs
stopped croaking and crept back into
the damp jungle.

Wanna crept between Tom and
Jamie, his eyes fixed on the deserted
lake. The boys followed his glance.
A grey wall of thick shimmery haze
was creeping across the water, blotting
out the sun. It was the middle of the
day, but it looked like twilight.

'This is spooky!' Jamie whispered.
'Something weird is going on . . .'

CHAPTER 4

A thick cloud of greenish-white fog billowed around them and swallowed them up.

'It's just hot, wet air,' Tom said. 'It must be atmospheric.'

'Eh?' Jamie was struggling to see anything in the milky light.

'It's a change in the weather, fossil brain,' Tom said. 'That would explain why the buffies flew off *and* why Wanna's been so upset. Animals know when a storm is coming.'

'Were there storms in the Triassic?'
Jamie wondered, re-opening the Fossil
Finder and typing in TRIASSIC WEATHER.

' "NORMALLY DRY, BUT WITH OCCASIONAL
VIOLENT STORMS FOLLOWED BY
FLASH FLOODING," ' he read.
He looked at Tom.

'Uh oh!' they said together.

A fork of lightning crackled
through the haze, lighting up the lake

Uh oh!?

for a split second and a great
boom of thunder crashed overhead.
Just in time, Jamie stowed the Fossil
Finder in his backpack as rain
began to hammer down.

Wanna raced into the
forest and took cover
under a broad leaf
fern. Jamie and Tom
squeezed in beside
him, holding up
the edges of the
huge leaf.

'This is proper
rain, not the
drizzle we get in
Dino Cove,' Tom
said, as they watched
the huge drops of rain make
dents in the ground where they fell.

'At least it's clearing
the fog a bit,' Jamie said,
peering out. Above him, the
leaf began to sag as the rain
formed a pool on the top of it.

z...z...z... *zap!*

A bolt of lightning zapped down on
the lake shore in front of them. Wanna
leapt to his feet with a grunk of alarm,
bumping his head on the leaf. The leaf tilted
and *sploosh!* the pool of water poured
down on Tom and Jamie.

'Urrgh!' Jamie spluttered.
He glanced at Tom. His
friend looked like a
drowned rat.

'Thanks,
Wanna,' Tom
groaned.

'At least we can't get any wetter, now.'

'Wrong!' Jamie told him. 'It's raining so hard that the ground can't soak it up.' He pointed to the water lapping around his feet. 'The lake's flooding! We've gotta get out of here, fast.'

'We'll be safer on higher ground,' Tom agreed. 'Head for the Red Mountains.'

The boys and Wanna splashed towards the foothills of the mountains. Here and there, they stepped in hollows where water

came up as high as Tom's and Jamie's knees.
Wanna stumbled on a trailing vine and
fell over with a splash. He lay on his side,
thrashing his legs.

'Don't panic; it's not that deep!' Jamie
laughed, as he and Tom hauled the spluttering
dinosaur to his feet. 'We're nearly out of it
now.'

Jamie led the way towards a dried up river
bed that cut through the red rocks.

'This gully looks the easiest way to climb
up,' he told Tom and Wanna.

High above
their heads,
a pair
of buffies
swept up the
mountainside
and disappeared
into the murky haze.

'The buffies are heading up the mountain for shelter, too,' Tom noticed.

They trudged up the gully, bending their heads against their chests to shield them from the driving rain.

In the distance, there was an ominous rumble. Wanna grunked in alarm.

'More thunder!' Jamie said, narrowing his eyes against the rain as he looked into the sky. 'Strange, I didn't see any lightning this time.'

Tom's eyes were fixed on the mountainside as the rumble grew louder and louder. 'It's not thunder!' he yelled. 'Something's coming our way!'

Jamie looked up to see
a wall of muddy red water
packed with fallen branches
and broken rock break
through the haze.

The torrent roared
down the gully towards
them.

CHAPTER 5

'Get climbing, quick!' Tom yelled.

He and Jamie hauled themselves up onto a rocky ledge and grabbed hold of Wanna's scaly arms. The little dinosaur scrabbled at the wet rocks, desperately trying to get a grip with his hind feet. Tom and Jamie pulled him up beside them just as the raging water swept over the place where they had just been standing.

Jamie wiped the rain out of his eyes. 'The rocks are too steep and slippery for Wanna to

climb,' he said with a frown. 'We'll have to stick to this ledge . . . if we can,' he added, as rainwater gushed over his feet. Rain was cascading down the red mountain like a waterfall, sploshing over the narrow rocky shelf.

'I thought hunting pterosaurs would be a nice, safe thing to do in Dino World, for once,' Tom murmured, as they edged along.

'Nice, and safe . . . and dry,' Jamie muttered. 'How wrong were we?' Rain poured off the end of his nose as he concentrated on placing one foot in front of the other on the slippery red rock. 'Let's hope the buffies have found somewhere to shelter from this storm.'

There was a crackle of lightning and the dark sky lit up with a blinding flash of light.

Boooom!

The thunder rolled. *Grunk!*

Wanna shrieked in alarm.

Jamie whirled round. There was no sign of their prehistoric friend. Jamie's stomach turned over as he looked down at the steep drop into the rushing water.

'Wanna's fallen over the edge!' he gasped, feeling like he was going to throw up.

Grunk! Grunk! Grunk!

Wanna's bony head peered out from behind the curtain of water that was pouring down the mountain, then disappeared again.

'He hasn't fallen off; he's fallen through!' Tom sounded as relieved as Jamie felt. 'There must be a cave behind here.' Tom stuck his

hand into the torrent. Sure enough, he
couldn't feel any rock.

'Here goes!' Tom shoulder-barged the
curtain of water and disappeared. Jamie
charged after him into the sheeting rain
and then a dark, dry cavern.

Wanna greeted them with a grunk
and a wag of his tail.

'He's pleased to be out of the rain,' Tom said.

'He's not the only one.' Jamie shook the
raindrops out of his eyes and flicked on his
torch. They were in a domed cavern the size
of his dad's dinosaur museum. The floor of the
cave was covered with a thick layer of dark
gritty stuff. It smelt like a mixture of
cow manure and bleach.

'Poo!' Jamie gasped,
shining his torch into
the cave. A wall of eyes
sparkled back at him.

'Buffy poo,' Tom agreed. 'There's gotta be a whole colony of buffies in here.'

Jamie slowly directed the beam of light round the cave. There were hundreds and hundreds of them, perched on every ledge and

every rock. They were watching the boys and
Wanna with fierce beady eyes. They rustled
their leathery wings and snapped their fanged
beaks as the torchlight fell on them.

'Some of them have babies,' Jamie hissed.
'They'll attack us if they think we're a threat.
Maybe we'll be safer outside in the storm.'

'We'll be OK if we turn off the torch and
keep very still and quiet,' Tom murmured,
'like when we watched the lighthouse bats.'

Jamie snapped off his torch. As his

eyes adjusted to the dim light that filtered through the curtain of water over the mouth of the cave, he could see that the buffies were settling down. Tom slowly took a few steps into the cave and sat down on a mound of dried buffy poo. Jamie did the same, and Wanna crept in and curled up on the ground beside them.

The pterosaurs soon forgot that they were there. Tom and Jamie watched, fascinated as they flitted from crevice to crevice, feeding their babies and squabbling over the best perches.

The boys were so absorbed in pterosaur-watching that the time flew by. Jamie suddenly realized the cave was growing lighter. The waterfall over the cave mouth had slowed to a drip.

'The sun's come out,' he said in surprise.

'We'd better be getting back,' Tom said, slowly standing up.

'Bye, buffies,' Jamie whispered, as he and Tom crept towards the mouth of the cave. He glanced back. Wanna was still fast asleep.

'Wake up, Wanna,' Jamie hissed loudly. 'We're off.'

Wanna leapt to his feet with a startled grunk and whirled round. His tail brushed past a buffy's nest.

Snap!

The buffy's fangs
closed on the tip of
Wanna's tail.

Grunk!

Wanna squealed. He
raced round and round,
thrashing his tail.

Grunk! Grunk!

In his panic, he slipped on a gritty pile
of fresh buffy poo and landed on his back,
kicking his feet and grunking loudly.

There was a loud rustling as the pterosaurs
took to the air. They swarmed up to the roof
of the cave, beating their wings. The cave
echoed with clicks and high pitched squeaks.

Then suddenly, one after another, the
buffies swooped down from the cave ceiling,
snapping their beaks.

'They're attacking Wanna!' Jamie yelled.

Jamie looked up. The bullies weren't
attacking. They were swarming out of the

CHAPTER 6

Jamie and Tom threw themselves over the little dinosaur's scaly tummy to protect him from the swooping pterosaurs. Jamie held his breath, waiting to feel the pecks of the buffies' sharp beaks on his neck. Instead, wind from their beating wings rustled his hair, and something sticky rained down on him.

Jamie looked up. The buffies weren't attacking. They were swarming out of the cave into the bright sunshine.

'It's OK, we're safe!' he told the others as he jumped to his feet, shaking the sticky stuff off his head. Lumpy bits of fresh buffy poo sprayed everywhere.

Jamie, Tom, and Wanna stepped out onto the ledge. A beautiful double rainbow hung above the steaming Triassic forest, and beneath the rainbow the pterosaurs were looping and swooping through the cloudy blue sky.

'They're not bumping into each other,' Tom murmured, as they watched the buffies whirl upwards, then drop into a low dive in a dazzling flying display. 'Maybe they've got something like echo location . . .'

'Great acrobatics,' Jamie joked as the cloud of pterosaurs swept over their heads, and circled up into the sky.

71

They watched the buffies disappear into the distance, then began to clamber down the fast-drying rocks. The lake was even bigger now but most of the rest of the flood water had disappeared already. They stopped at the lake to wash off the buffy poo before they re-entered the steamy Triassic forest.

Water still
dripped from the
leaves and Wanna
gambolled ahead
of the boys, trying
to catch drops in his
mouth, as they made
their way back to the
hollow tree.

'Wanna's happy now the
storm's passed,' Tom grinned, as
their prehistoric playmate jumped on
a pine cone and gobbled it up.

'See you next time, Wanna,' Jamie said,
patting him on the nose.

Wanna wagged his tail as the boys fit their
feet into the fresh dinosaur tracks.

'Bye!' Tom and Jamie called, as they
stepped backwards towards the hollow tree
trunk. There was a flash of light like lightning

as the tracks turned to stone and they found themselves back in Dinosaur Cove once more.

The drizzle had stopped and twilight was falling as they reached the old lighthouse, wrapped up warm in their coats. Grandad was standing in the garden, gazing up into the sky.

'You missed the bats taking flight,' Grandad told them. 'You should've seen 'em flitting round the garden catching insects.' He looked wistful for a moment. 'There's a cave in Texas where thousands of bats roost and, when darkness falls, they swarm out like a huge cloud. It'd be really special to see something like that, wouldn't it?'

Jamie flicked a bit of dusty fossil buffy poo off his cheek and glanced at Tom.

'Awesome!' he agreed.

DINOSAUR WORLD

- - - - BOYS' ROUTE

Desert

N
W E
S

Oasis

Fertile
river

Ocean
That
way
⬇

76

Red Mountain

Forest

Dried out river bed

Hollow
Tree

Pond

Scrubland

GLOSSARY

Ammonite (am-on-ite) – an extinct animal with octopus-like legs and often a spiral-shaped shell that lived in the ocean.

Gingko (gink-oh) – a tree native to China called a 'living fossil' because fossils of it have been found dating back millions of years, yet they are still around today. Also known as the stink bomb tree because of its smelly apricot-like fruit.

Pipistrelle (pip-ist-ral) – a relatively common species of brown bat.

Postosuchus (poss-toh-suck-us) – this 4–5 metre long creature wasn't a dinosaur, but a close ancestor of today's crocodiles. Unlike crocodiles, its legs were tucked under its body and it had protective plates on its backs. It had large, sharp teeth and hunted its food.

Preondactylus Buffarini (pray-on-dak-til-us buff-ah-reen-ee) – a type of pterosaur with a long tail and short wings. It was discovered by a scientist named Buffarini in what is now Italy.

Pterosaur (ter-oh-sor) – a prehistoric flying reptile. Its wings were leathery and light and some of these 'winged lizards' had fur on their bodies and bony crests on their heads.

Triassic (try-as-sick) – from about 200 to 250 million years ago, during this time period, seed plants and spiney trees flourished on land along with many species of reptiles and, eventually, the first dinosaurs.

Wannanosaurus (wah-nan-oh-sor-us) – a dinosaur that only ate plants and used its hard, flat skull to defend itself. Named after the place it was discovered: Wannano in China.

Take care –
we're coming to steal you away

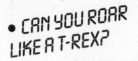